The Land of One-Armed Men

Nick Stump

The Land of One-Armed Men

Loose Canons Publishing

Loose Canons Publishing
A division of Creative Resources Inc.
550 West Kentucky Street
Louisville, KY 40203

Cover design by Dan Stewart
Cover photo by Ted Wathen/Quadrant
Typography by Just Your Type

First Edition Published 1993

ISBN 0-9634142-1-6

Printed in the United States of America

ACKNOWLEDGMENTS

To my mother and father, Alice and Albert Stamper. You gave me a home filled with hope and humor. I love you both.

To Brian and Marea. If a man's wealth is measured by the goodness of his children, then I am indeed rich.

Thanks and much love to my in-laws, Cova and Dee Lyle. You sure raised a wonderful daughter.

Thanks to Tracy and Richard Allen and to Carol Walker for all your help.

Special thanks to Lynne Cralle, Walter Harding, Marty Polio, Bob and Louise Schulman, and Bob Hill – good friends all.

Thank you, Dan Stewart!!

Special thanks to the Metropolitan Blues All-Stars – David White, Ricky Baldwin, Frank Schaap and Rodney Hatfield. True brothers are hard to find. I am much better for knowing you all.

Thanks to Frank Schaap, my longtime songwriting partner and pal. It's been a great twenty years.

Thanks to Rodney Hatfield both for your example and your unfailing support of this effort. It means everything to me.

Thanks to the folks at the Bell House.

To my wife, Bonnie McCafferty, you give me encouragement, understanding and help. Every day I thank God for you. You are the woman of my dreams.

Finally, to Drs. Richard and Lawrence Jelsma. You saved my wife's life. I am eternally grateful.

To my wife, Bonnie McCafferty.
You are my treasure.
All my love.

Y.B.F.

TABLE OF CONTENTS

DRINKING FROM THE BEGGAR'S CUP

THE LAND OF ONE-ARMED MEN

SONGS FROM THE BOOK OF REVELATIONS

Drinking From The Beggar's Cup

Billy O

doomed
post-modernist
guitarslinger
shot through the heart
by Nora
feminist dancer
waitress
enduring her pre-suburban period

They patched him up
lying,
"only a flesh wound"
and sent him back
to the road

We saw him no more
nothing but dusty letters
posted to the house
where love used to live

May All Her Dreams Come True

She came out of the hills
in the stale belly of a Greyhound
hungry for pretty things
beauty pins,
brass beds,
pants suits,
cross your heart brassieres,
all those treasures
a good man would have bought her

She took a job at the electric company
worked hard
got ahead
married a good man the second time
and made him the instrument of her ambition

I always admired her
she was wise in the way
she kept her second husband
afraid of her

Left Me

She left me, he cried
tears pulsing down
the worn gullies
of his face

What did you expect?
I thought
but I knew his hurt would not
heal with a salve of guilt
smoothed on by a mean friend

My memory was fresh
Before it was my tears
and he bought me drinks
and took my side
though we both knew
I didn't have one

So, we had drinks
and I took his side
and cursed women
and love
and hope
and waited for the time
when he could go home
to face the cold bed
and the silent telephone

Frank

Guitar tattoo artist
fills up my left ear
shows me where to step
not so fancy
as to hide the beat

Girls in
faded housedresses
sway to the
insistent drone
of that old wooden
guitar

He knows secrets
about those girls
about that old
guitar

It's the same secret
Frank always knows where
the beat is

Skid Marks

Her leaving
opened a hole
in his gut
big enough
to echo
the black scream
of an overloaded coal truck

Bonded bourbon
and the blue pills
from the VA
could not soothe the burn
or blot up the skid marks

Big Buddy

rolls big delicious
Drum cigarettes
the white faced
college girls
with their red pouts
and berets
come around sometime
to smoke his big delicious cigarettes
and get some experience

He serves soupbeans
yellow cornbread
and plays old records that
pop and crack over the
snap of his fingers

One morning
the white-faced girls gone
Big Buddy
looks in the mirror
and decides
that it's time
to call
The Hair Club For Men

Love Letter

He wrote her from Eddyville and sent his picture and she thought he had nice handwriting even if his spelling was off sometimes but that was OK cause he was the best body man in the Midwest and when he got out they were going to go together and buy some land outside town. People would come from town to get him to work on their cars. They would drive that far to get the best work, besides she had her job at Wal-Mart to help out til they got on their feet, then she could quit her job and just do the books for him. They were going to have three babies, though talk about the babies almost broke them up before he got out of the pen. He wanted two boys and a girl and she wanted two girls and a boy and he said that they needed boys cause boys could work in the body shop and girls couldn't. She said that girls could too work in the body shop if they wanted, but that her girls would be working in the beauty shop and he said what beauty shop? And she said I'm going to BEAUTICIAN college and open up a beauty shop next door to the body shop – that way women could come and get their hair done while he was painting their car and he said it was the dumbest idea he ever heard and then he hung up on her and there was no way for her to call him back and it made her mad, and hurt her feelings even worse because she had accepted the charges for the phone call and felt that if anyone got to hang up on someone it ought to be the one who was paying for the call.

That night she wrote him a letter and told him just that, but he didn't call and no letter came for three weeks and she thought she might go crazy so she wrote him and told him that they could have three boys if he wanted and that all she cared about was when he was getting out of the pen cause she missed him even though she had only known him for six months and had never really been with him and wasn't there anything that could be done to prove that he was an INNOCENT man. He wrote back and said it was OK with him if she wanted a beauty shop and maybe they ought to have six kids, three of each and that way everybody would be happy, but she said with that many kids they wouldn't have any time for romance and he laughed and said, "Where do you think those six kids will come from?" She blushed right there in her room by herself listening to him talk like that. Before they hung up he asked her to send him a carton of Marlboros and told her that he loved her. She whispered back, "I love you too . . ." He wasn't like other convicts she had written before, of course she had never been engaged to any of them and he was her first murderer.

Love

Daddy talks to all the men
Daddy never thinks of sin
He hits Momma when I'm asleep
I lay there and never peep

Supper's late or not at all
I stay out and play some ball
I wash my face and go to school
my Momma didn't raise no fool

White coats took my Momma away
Now she's gone she'll have to stay
Momma comes home she'll act real good
Just like Daddy said she should

Now Momma cries most of the time

singing, Love sure ain't no nursery rhyme
Love sure ain't no nursery rhyme
Love sure ain't no nursery rhyme
Love sure ain't no nursery rhyme

Drinking From The Beggar's Cup

His knees worn thin and sore
from all the times he pleaded
with her to take him back just
one more time and I'll be good
and how he didn't have trouble
with drinking it was just that
sometimes bad things happened
to good people and she told her
girlfriend that he was a good
man but that sometimes he acted
like a asshole but he's good
you'll like him once you get to
know him

I think she liked him drunk better
anyway cause when he quit yelling
and hitting she always knew he would
be real sorry and it was almost the
same as love being real real sorry
and she could keep him sorry most of
the night if she just wouldn't give in
and forgive him too soon

Sometimes they would be mad and sorry
for the whole night and he would pat her and
pay attention saying how good she looked
how smart she was and he would cook her
his famous Italian dinner and bring it
to her with a flower on the tray

I always knew they were having trouble
when I went over and they were eating
spaghetti and he was drinking Coke
from the beggar's cup

Werewife

I dreamed you had two big teeth
laying over your low fat lip
a changeling
werewife

Why was I so surprised
when I awoke
to find you drinking
the last few drops of my soul

Schoolboy

(For Darrin Van Horn)

They called him schoolboy
but he sure did hurt that man
He reached down
pulled his gutsnake
and he hurt that man
the man was big
He remembered his gutsnake

But the snake lives only with boys
who stand in the fire
looking ringside
for that woman
with the yes-look
in her eyes

Love Times Three

Jimmy Lee
got cut dead
in the backseat
of a black transam
over a sorry woman
who is probably out
right now
trying to get another man
killed

Jack Samson
took a gun and
fired it right
through his heart
over a woman
who now
twenty years later
couldn't hold his
interest for five minutes

Baby Jones
had her stomach
stapled and in four months
ate so little that
she starved to death
in her own home

She was just
trying to become
the kind of woman
a man would die for

Three Little Words

red drunk ugly
ham bone fist
beat wife blue
bust her dish
make kid cry
lose your job
lose your home
ain't you grand
red drunk ugly

Tori

Our dog
big and tan
leaves his hair
on the brown
underfoot
He has been here
for 89 years (dogstyle)

When we make love
He stands outside
our room
making safe these
profound moments
of weakness

Though I am new
He knows me and
comes to my voice
We walk the park
cold and close

My wife tells me
Tori is here to
demonstrate love
no matter what

and to teach us
how to grieve

Neuro I.C.U.

Rain doesn't fall in sheets
but descends in plumes
there is nothing orderly
sheetlike in this rain

We know order here
nurses come every half-hour
to poke, and stick
to access

Their easy, friendly manner
seems contrary to this
grim situation

Two more days til the operation
my wife seems unafraid
I think she lies
so I lie too
We say it will be alright
that we're not afraid

They give her another shot
for pain
and then they leave

My wife sleep twists
in sheets of cotton
Outside the rain
falls in plumes

Operation

They sent word upstairs
she made it
a success
hope where there was
so little
my heart raced
could there be one good ending
to this sad story

I rode the elevator downstairs
and took my smoke
in the second story
of the parking garage
Outside heat hung over me like
a black hangmans hood
but underneath it was cooler
and full of birds
sparrows, finches, cardinals
I looked over the trees
to a tower in the distance
pointing to the heavens

She's alive!
I yelled
as loud as I could
and the word "alive"
bounced around the concrete

Behind me
over me
around all sides of me
replied
a chorus of birdsongs

Smoking in the Dark

Late night whispered love songs
lying side by side
twice burned fires–now banked
smoulder

Two red eyes glow
as we, now easy and
astride our new found secret
murmur sweet somethings

If I would be your dancing cowboy
and you my baby
I could hold you close
against winter's touch

Tonight, all our love
lies side by side
smoking in the dark

The Land of One-Armed Men

A. F. Stamper, USN

He shaved his head
and oiled it
as they couldn’t stay clean

He made their skullbust
from raisins and sugar
stole from the army

He painted a cigar box black
and pointed like a camera
at willing Filipino girls

He threw pink 50 caliber ribbons
into the sky but
never knew if they landed

One bright blue afternoon
a Jap Zero aimed
and dived right
for him
but we finally knocked
him down, he said

His tears fell down
his face
into
his smile

Boy With The 20th Maine

He died on a hillside
in 1863, leaving no one
to weep
No woman
to take his name
or hold his hands
to her breasts
and show
him girl secrets

The only bits
left of him were
two brass buttons
kicked up by a sullen boy
in short pants
with his father
walking the fields
on vacation
in Gettysburg

Ned

Uncle Ned
died in the war
in Panama
A gun exploded
or he got cut
by a sad-eyed
ladies man
I heard both stories

The first time I saw him
was a picture
(school days 1937)
he looked exactly like me

Before the war
He played guitar,
yodeled
and hid in the woods
from his daddy

One night
my mother told me
he wasn't dead
but alive
swinging through the jungle
like Tarzan
his body golden and pure

That night
I wished it were true
so he could tell my mother
Not to cry

Flashback

Asian doctors
Crying babies
Gaping holes blown
in yellow mud
Hillsides gone
Rivers dead
Hueys criss-cross
the narrow sky

Camouflage men
clean guns while
their hungry wives
dream of life
in America

Every day
Eastern Kentucky
looks
a little more
like
Vietnam

Disappearing Act *(In Memory of Belinda Mason)*

"I'm disappearing."
Her words
barely pushing
electrons through
the wire between us

The Great Hillbilly Woman
Disappearing Act

Poof!

Gone . . .

Leaving nothing but
children and memories

Wingtips

Yellow graveyard mud
slops up on my carefully
shined black wingtips
They look just like
my father's shoes

What a terrible thing it is
to be a man
We stand here
the six of us
with him alone

They made us carry him
to the graveyard
and we stand there
looking at his widow
hearing the preacher drone on

We say nothing
acting like this is a perfectly
normal adult situation
Never letting on
that we want to
drop the box
and run away
screaming

Duststorm in Indiana

In the great blue van
they travel across
the great Midwest
Ohio, Indiana
Bandannaed mouths
on a macabre trail drive
of starving cattle
broken bones
no ammunition

Somewhere in the mocking scorch
between Kokomo and Dayton
dust demons dance
to a frenzy
and mirror the jig
of his own devils

Inside that slow moving
blistering blue ruin
he sits – dispirited
dreams dying
dirt in his mouth
not quite enough
hot whiskey
to wash away
the taste of defeat

Roadhouse Door Sign

No Helmets
No Colors
No Gambling
No Dope
No Fighting
No Niggers
No Outside Liquor
Tables For Ladies

Deja Boo

I dreamed
of burning airplanes
sliding into the wet green
of Laos
"SAMs up!!"
Yelling into the darkness
like a hundred
nights before

I hear him say
"We're going in."
Then nothing
but red crackle
over the earphones

Twenty years later
I jerk awake
insides hot, watery
light my cigarette
off the last one
no whiskey
to wash down my sleep
I sit by the window
scared
listening to cars
pass by
Forest Avenue

Slow Night Somewhere Outside Orlando

In a strip mall
every store lettered
hot red
between
Suzy's Clip and Curl
and Kill Zone Tae Kwon Do
a real blues bar
dirty floor
piss
old beer

Outside
the owner
stiff white shirt
club tie
checks his watch
more often than
he needs to

The band
all aging white men
blows a keening
blue snake
through
the thick air

The dance floor is
crowded and filled
with an uncommon number
of big women
They scowl
and grind their hips
in slow motion

Three shows
in a state where
time has stopped
Nick Stump is having
a slow night
somewhere outside Orlando

The Land of One-Armed Men

How many were they?
Every house
had one or two
those maimed
tore up
tore down
hacking black
stumbling by
on broken feet

How many fingers does it
take to make a pie
How many arms,
legs, hands
and hearts?
How many eyes?

In coal mines, lumberyards,
on bad roads, in war,
floods, on tractors,
and in desperate marriages

We pay for our
time here
piece by piece

Elvis on Rodeo Drive

Elvis rides low
on the black concrete
hair pomped
like Tony Curtis
Hungry

The shopkeepers
on Rodeo Drive
smile because
they all know
a secret

The shopkeepers
on Rodeo Drive
stock
black leather
gold belts
silver sunglasses
        and
Sweetpotato pie

The shopkeepers
on Rodeo Drive
smile because
they know
the King is coming

They
prepare his house
before him

Eating

We sit in Shoney's
the band
eagerly looking
over the menu
this meal looked
forward to since breakfast

I know
that Frank will only order brown food
that David will have two entrees
that Ricky will eat a turkey sandwich
and that Rodney will get the wrong order

We know the menu
and the food
and each other
Yet we are happy to be there
it is the only break
from the torpor of the day

Sitting With The Dying

She sits up with the dying
blotting tears
holding blue veined hands
that tighten with the pain

She rubs backs
pushes morphine buttons
Once she gave her best friend
that extra big shot
to help her along the way

Sometimes they come around
after her tv's off the air
and her husband's snoring
in the other room

They spread their black wings
and ride the damp river breeze
over her trailer
just to see how she's doing

Duck

I read about you in the paper
how you came home in a flag-draped box
over twenty years ago
I felt unsettled
It was the first I had heard

They said you were killed outside
Saigon and that everyone was just
heartsick

They buried you on the hill
behind your Daddy's house
up there with the miners and
unnamed babies

I always intended to get in touch
but time and distance kept me away
But I wondered if you ever married
that skinny girl from over in Perry
County or did you move away like me

It's hard to believe that you're home
on that hill
still eighteen

The End Of An Era

Thin-haired, gun nut
Bob the Lonely Communist
sits behind the counter
at the Spaghetti Junction 7-Eleven
As he sells dry long johns
and turns on gas pumps
he mulls over his days in Africa
with the State Department
He would do anything to get back
        Anything . . .

He lives with a big German woman
Behind her back we call her Frau Rump
but we are only being kind
She eats boiled potatoes, cabbage
and big cheap sausages
"American food is no good."
She tells me every time I see her

She talks constantly about the reunification
"Adolf Hitler was an excellent organizer."
"If he could be kept on a leash, there would
be room for Hitler in the New Germany."

Sometimes, full of cabbage and thin beer
she dreams of damp Argentine nights
Across the table sits the young Führer
His bare foot slides up her damp silk dress
as he raises his glass in a silent toast

In the background she can hear
the sound of train after train
departing
precisely
on time

Pop

Charlie Gabbard
Fought in World War One
Got shot
Got gassed
Rode in the horse cavalry
Kicked the shit out of the Kaiser
and caught the clap in Gay Pareeˊ

Charlie Gabbard
Worked for the government
Sired children he didn't like
Drank whiskey on the porch
Got mean
Got sick
and retired to a trailer park in Florida

Charlie Gabbard
Smoked Pall Malls
Drank Old Crow
Spit at his neighbors
Gave me my first whiskey
and laughed when his twelve gauge
knocked me down

Charlie Gabbard
Fished for Sheepshead
Cursed the Democrats
Voted for Kennedy
Made bows and arrows
Cursed the communists
Claimed he knew Ernest Hemingway
Got drunk and told me about
the whores in Pareeˊ

Charlie Gabbard
Listened to the shortwave
Made me sing "Pretty Saro"
Made me eat raw oysters
Hated Lawrence Welk
Sneaked off to Cuba
and caught the clap in gay Havana

Charlie Gabbard
Got older
Drank more Old Crow
Got meaner
Got sicker
and died begging his wife
for one more good time

Staff Sgt. Lewis

Jack Lewis
rode in the rear
of the plane
and upon landing
in Udorn
with a hard bump
the tail broke off
he fell out
and was smeared
all over the runway

He left one ex-wife
two sons
a set of parents
and a whore
standing outside
the main gate
waiting to go
to the PX

Jimbo

We drank beer on the river
and threw rocks to break
the still emerald surface
We didn't fish except once
with dynamite

Mostly we drank warm tall boys
sweet brown half-pints
and talked about girls
In our new friendship
we were each eager
to believe the other's lies

A year later he was back
from Vietnam
dead and not looking
like himself at all
his momma said it was
a mistake – the wrong boy

But it was him
bad color, flat face
drained and stuffed
into a green PFC's suit

The honor guard was up
from Ft. Knox
seven men, three shots apiece
The sound echoed off
the hill across from
the family graveyard

Later their Corporal looked
down at the river
and asked me about the fishing

Shiloh

Dawn in Tennessee
before the sun
still except for
the expectant chatter of
mourning birds
we walk the green meadow

Underneath our feet
the rattle and rumble
of cannonballs
the tinkle of loose equipment
the scour of sabers
the buzz of miniballs
the click of dead men's teeth
Whispering

Don't Sleep Too Late

This morning as I slept later than I should
later than was good for me
Caught in that sleep time
when pain and thirst
scratch deep gouges in your rest
I dreamed they shot the President
on TV during prime time

Neilson ratings were lower
than expected
seventy six percent
of us
were watching the
last episode
of
Cheers

Thanksgiving Memory

Silver bottle tipped
to face the morning
Whiskey sick
I cursed the bird
slick and heavy

Dry meat
friends by obligation
one more open bottle
No grace said
No thanks given

Imagine

(for Irvin Hatfield)

Imagine that
you crawl on your belly
in a coal seam
over a mile underground
There is exactly thirty-two inches
between the roof and the floor

The air is full of black dust
that gets into your skin, mouth
and lungs and every day
you wonder if the roof
will fall

You don't see the sun for nine months
and your oldest boy told you last week
that only a fool would work in the mines

Sometimes you wake up
in the middle of the night
terrified that it's already time to go to work
and when it's not time you lay there unable to
go back to sleep

You try to tell your children
about the American Dream
but they look at the black under your fingernails
and don't believe a word you're saying

If you don't die in a roof fall, or an explosion
or get electrocuted
If your mine stays open long enough
for you to retire
You will find yourself at a hearing
where some Mercedes-driving lawyer
says the black sputum you hack up each day
has nothing at all to do
with the forty years
you spent on your knees

Imagine that

King

At the home
his children put the bird feeder
right outside his window
(he loves his birds)
they whispered

This man once
drove a team of oxen
up Torrent Hill
through the middle of a tornado
and could whip two men
at once

The last time I saw him
he sat in the rec room
with other deposed kings
painting a ceramic wildcat blue
remembering bits and pieces

Jo Jo

Jo Jo the dog-faced boy
looked in the mirror
a long time
thinking of the
laughing, leering
mudhole of humanity
who came night after night
to see his face
He turned away from
his image
feeling not in the least
like man's best friend

Artifacts

My mother walks the new plowed fields
behind old red no name tractors
and sometimes a shiny green John Deere
Her eyes scan the ground
like the hunting bird she is

They let her come to the fields
even the one who lets no one else
She is careful of the dirt
and the new tobacco
seeking only the flint
made by brown hands
long dead

On a sweet May morning
after a rain
She says, It's a real good day
the rain washes away the dust
so we can see the points
The ground is turned
I smell the strong rot
of childhood gardens

Over there on that high spot!
She points toward the brown river
They made their camp there
close to the water
For one clear moment I see
through her old eyes
this piece of ground
before it was a field
before John Deere tractors

Behind her back
her neighbors call her
Squaw Woman
She knows what they say
but the name suits her
and she likes it

War Stories

Tell me about the war, Daddy
And he would
making stories
about getting drunk
about stolen jeeps
and the whores

I wanted to know about
guns, heroes, and death
He didn't say much then
just that everyone did
their job and that there
weren't any heroes

I was always disappointed
with the lack of adventure
in his tales

Twenty years later
in my safe, dark bedroom
here in Kentucky
a mortar round lands
right on my head
and I wake up

Today I will disappoint my child
with tales
of getting drunk
stolen jeeps
and whores

It is the father's
duty to never
tell the truth

Great Uncle

My great uncle
But a small man
the only arm left
was his right
a crane accident
“mashed my arm
so flat it didn’t
bleed
a teacup full.”

In my family
success is
often measured
by how little
we bleed

Word From The Edge Of The Earth

They be devils out here
this boiled blood sea
lies still and flat
beyond the horizon

I pull lines
hoisting hope
praying for wind to
blow this ship east
to the blue of
my wife's kind eyes
They be devils out here

Lost John

Lost John
left his leg
moldering
in the Aragonne Forest

It lay there in a yellow
gas pocket
listening
to the cries
of lost momma's boys

The third of November 1961
after his check came
after the bootlegger
after John took his first
half-pint
He told me
"My leg ain't in France
No, it's up in heaven
Waiting for the rest of me."
Somehow, that picture gave me
little comfort

The Last Wolf in Eastern Kentucky

(For Rodney)

Sighted up on Buffalo
all ribs, fur and eyes
dogged by a pack
of four-wheeling
wild-eyed men
Finally, cornered
her breath short
burning like death
she looked into
the guns
and in moments, dead

They brought her to town
lashed across the front
of a new, yellow Blazer
like some gory hood ornament
and left her in front
of the courthouse
so all could see

That night all cows
    we didn't have
on all the farms
    we didn't have
and all the chickens
    we didn't have
in all the hen houses
    we didn't have
They could all
sleep quietly
    Safe
from the last wolf
in Eastern Kentucky

Songs From the Book of Revelations

Riding To A Shallow Grave

Daddy's gone a riding
Pistol in his hand
No one could dissuade him
On his way to the promised land
Had a sweethearted woman
Riding by his side
Too young to be a widow
Too old to be a bride

(Chorus)
Oh the children that he knew
Don't know the stories
From the true
The bounty he brought home
Was all the love he gave
Daddy's gone a riding to a shallow grave

Ten little children, called after his name
It's not a tragedy
It's a crying shame
There's a death bell sounding
No warning it gave
Daddy's gone a riding to a shallow grave

She saved his letter
Said soon I'm coming home
No one could replace you
I'm riding all the way alone
Tell all the children
I'm coming back to stay
Soon as I do my job
Standing on Judgment Day

Storm Coming Through

Somebody call me
Tell me I'm all right
Somebody call me
I'm afraid of the night
I heard the rumble of thunder
I shivered when the wind blew
I know in my heart
There's a storm coming through

Somebody call me
I'm here all alone
Somebody call me
I'm staring at the telephone
I heard her whisper goodbye
Now my tears run true
I know in my heart
There's a storm coming through

(Chorus)
Yesterday my eyes were dry
Sun was shining not a cloud in the sky
I said don't go
She said I can't stay
Now the storm's coming through
Gonna wash me away
Somebody call me

Trying Times

Daddy's got his new cane
Said things will never be the same
Making love's just a memory
You know the same thing'll happen to you and me

My wife didn't even fight
She said that woman won't treat you right
You're gonna wake up cold one night
And want to be alone with me

(Chorus)
These are trying times
These are trying times
These are trying times
And I'm trying to get back home

If I could get a new car
You know Hazard ain't very far
But no matter who you think you are
Don't forget the way back home

My son said he couldn't stay
Eighteen years of missed birthdays
Said he'd call me on the telephone
But that he had to get back home

Where's Santa Claus

There's smoke in the air
Fires are burning
Times are tough
There's no hope in sight
The man walking down the street
You know he's got a yearning
For a warm bed to sleep in tonight

(Chorus)
Daddy's lost his job,
Got nothing to do
Mama's trying to talk him up,
But she's feeling blue
They got three kids
They don't know how to feed them
Where's Santa Claus when we need him

There's children under cover
But they don't cry
Cause there ain't no babies in this war
Somebody's knocking
But they won't answer
Cause it ain't Santa standing at the door

Father at the mission
Bible in his hand
God knows all the things he's tried
He lost his faith, praying for a miracle
Cause he can't stand to see those hungry eyes

Where's Santa Claus
    up on the Eastside
Where's Santa Claus
    he's the rich man's friend
All those hungry people
    no way to feed them
Where's Santa Claus when we need him

Daddy Sleeps On The Arizona

(For My Father)

The month of December, 1941
Letter came from the President
Said we're sorry to inform you
That's when Momma started crying
And she told us kids just what that letter meant

(Chorus)
She said
Your Daddy sleeps on the Arizona
He's dreaming in the blue, blue sea
Daddy sleeps on the Arizona
And he's dreaming of you and me

Black bordered newspapers all over town
Long, sad roll calls of the dead
Momma showed me my Daddy's name
Saying life will never be the same
And the tears run down Momma's face
And she said

Your Daddy sleeps on the Arizona
Dreaming in the blue, blue sea
Daddy sleeps on the Arizona
And he's a'dreaming there
Of you and of me

Now I'm a whole lot older
Than my Daddy ever got to be
Momma's getting old and feeling blue
You can see my Daddy's grave
Underneath the flag that he died to save
He's sleeping there for me and for you

On a Creek Called Troublesome

Three kids sleeping on the hillside
Hope can't make the corn green
Old horse broke down
So here's where we had to stay
Run high springtide
Run high wash away the hillside
No hope on a creek called Troublesome
Can't see the sky

Brother went down to the canefields
Died for a crossroads
Now I hate to see
The evening sun go down
Sing high oh whippoorwill
Sing low and lie so still
No hope on a creek called Troublesome
Can't see the sky

(Chorus)
Remember the day you left Virginia
Riding on a two dollar horse
Couldn't keep your powder dry
Now there's no one to defend you
No love on a creek called Troublesome
Can't see the sky

Bad Situation

Yes, I walk with the King of Fools
I drink water from a muddy pool
Nobody left still knows my name
I got nobody left to blame
Talking 'bout a bad situation
Talking 'bout a bad situation
Talking 'bout a bad situation going on

Promised never to be apart
Then you went and broke my heart
Now I'm wondering what to do
You left me crying boo hoo hoo
Talking 'bout a bad situation
Talking 'bout a bad situation
Talking 'bout a bad situation going on

Yes my mother said to me
Said her Lord could set me free
But I still walk with the King of Fools
I crave water from a muddy pool
Talking 'bout a bad situation
Talking 'bout a bad situation
Talking 'bout a bad situation going on

Devil Gets His Due

He sold out to the Devil
But he didn't get enough
Left his wife and baby
For a little ol' piece of fluff
Now he's crying, learning how to sing the blues
And he knows the Devil always gets his due

No matter how much whiskey
There's a thirst he cannot slake
Desperation sleeping in his bed
While he sits up awake
And the Trying Times have just begun
Now he knows it's true
He knows the Devil always gets his due

(Chorus)
Gets his due
Gets his due
You thought they were lying
Now you know it's true
Now your day is over
There's nothing left for you
And you know the Devil always gets his due

Six and twenty women
Praying for my soul
Though I rode the highway
I never paid the toll
Singing "Hey, Hey Hosanna"
Really in the spirit true
Cause they know thc Devil gets his due

Deep Mine Blues

(with Lionel Delmore and Frank Schaap)

I knew before I was a man
I'd not go down in the mines
Like my dad and his dad and friends by the score
Who are crippled and bent at the spine

(Chorus)
You never see the light of day
You can't wash that coal dust away
You'll never gain as much as you lose
When you're singing those deep mine blues

Down in the city, jobs they were few
Back home they needed some men
They put me on digging Number Nine Coal
Alongside my kinfolk and friends

(Chorus)
You never see the light of day
You can't wash that coal dust away
You'll never gain as much as you lose
When you're singing those deep mine blues

(Bridge)
Sing it high
Sing it low
Sing the song however you choose
You go to work when the whistle blows
And you're singing them deep mine blues

Dead Man Walking

Judge said justice be done
Somebody lost, Nobody won
The story's over tonight
Give an eye for an eye
Baby please don't cry
Time to stop that talking
Dead man walking

The priest outside my cell
Here to keep my spirit well
Only God knows where I been
Feel the last teardrop
Hear the last tick tock
Time to stop that talking
Dead man walking

(Chorus)
Yes, I know what it means to say I'm sorry
You heard me begging you please
But I'm a standup guy
Don't plan to fuss and cry
Don't need a ride, step aside
Dead man walking

There's no reason why
Too much whiskey, a blink of the eye
Now I'm eating ice cream and steak
Hear those footsteps coming
No place to do my running
Now there's nobody talking
Dead man walking

Night Patrol

Trying to get a ride
On Highway Fifteen
Coal truck driver almost run over me
I been gone – going toe to toe
You know I done my last night patrol

Standing in the rain
I'm thinking of you
My eastbound thumb just turned blue
Kept my ears open – kept my aim low
You know I done my last night patrol

(Chorus)
It's a long, long way to Kentucky
When you're coming from Saigon
You know I feel so very, very lucky
Standing here with these wet boots on

Got two thousand dollars
Some French perfume
Can't wait to see your face when I walk into the room
Got you a jade necklace and a red kimono
You know I done my last night patrol

Night Rider

What do you do when the crow's on the roof
You can hear your wife and children cry
Momma gone and fear's on the loose
Cause the nightrider's coming by and by

Doctor, Doctor, please let me lay down
Please don't make me go home
Bring that young woman to sit and hold my hand
I can't face that nightrider alone

(Chorus)
I'm so blue, blue, blue
I'm so blue, blue, blue
All my good memories are washing out to sea
There ain't nothing nobody can do

Carry me back to sweet Kentucky
Up where the Stillwater breezes blow
Don't tell anybody about the tears on my face
When you saw the nightrider go

Raging Heart

(with Frank Schaap)

A raging heart keeps her awake
She tosses and turns her body shakes
Tonight she's grieving for the better days
But a raging heart won't go away

He's gone all night from their bedroom
When he comes home she smells perfume
She thinks about leaving – love makes her stay
And a raging heart that won't go away

(Chorus)
She's stopped dreaming
Now she's gonna get even
She's got a pistol underneath her pillow
She's got a reason
When he comes home
She's gonna have her say
Cause a raging heart won't go away

When it falls to pieces she'll get the blame
Some call it sad, some a crying shame
Her last act of love – a price he'll pay
For a raging heart that won't go away
(repeat Chorus)